TAO
The Little Samurai

#2

Ninjas and Knock Outs!

Laurent Richard
illustrated by **Nicolas Ryser**
Translation: **Edward Gauvin**

GRAPHIC UNIVERSE™ • MINNEAPOLIS

STORY BY LAURENT RICHARD
ILLUSTRATIONS BY NICOLAS RYSER
TRANSLATION BY EDWARD GAUVIN

FIRST AMERICAN EDITION PUBLISHED IN 2014 BY GRAPHIC UNIVERSE™.

FARCES ET ATTAQUES! BY LAURENT RICHARD AND NICOLAS RYSER © BAYARD ÉDITIONS, 2011
PITRES ET DRAGONS! BY LAURENT RICHARD AND NICOLAS RYSER © BAYARD ÉDITIONS, 2011
COPYRIGHT © 2014 BY LERNER PUBLISHING GROUP, INC., FOR THE US EDITION

GRAPHIC UNIVERSE™ IS A TRADEMARK OF LERNER PUBLISHING GROUP, INC.

GRAPHIC UNIVERSE™
A DIVISION OF LERNER PUBLISHING GROUP, INC.
241 FIRST AVENUE NORTH
MINNEAPOLIS, MN 55401 U.S.A.

FOR READING LEVELS AND MORE INFORMATION,
LOOK UP THIS TITLE AT WWW.LERNERBOOKS.COM.

MAIN BODY TEXT SET IN CCWILDWORDS 8.5/10.5.
TYPEFACE PROVIDED BY FONTOGRAPHER.

LIBRARY OF CONGRESS CATALOGING-IN-PUBLICATION DATA

RICHARD, LAURENT, 1968-
   [FARCES ET ATTAQUES! ENGLISH.]
   NINJAS AND KNOCK OUTS! / BY LAURENT RICHARD; ILLUSTRATED BY NICOLAS RYSER ;
TRANSLATION, EDWARD GAUVIN. – FIRST AMERICAN EDITION.
   P.   CM. – (TAO, THE LITTLE SAMURAI ; #2)
   SUMMARY: TAO IS A STUDENT AT VENERABLE MASTER SNOW'S MARTIAL ARTS SCHOOL. WITH HIS FRIENDS RAY AND LEE AND HIS NOT-GIRLFRIEND KAT, HE TRIES TO FOLLOW THE TEACHINGS OF THE MASTERS AT THE SCHOOL–OR, MORE OFTEN, FINDS A WAY AROUND THE MASTERS' ADVICE. TAO DOES NOT LACK FOR AMBITION, BUT HE HAS A TENDENCY TO GET HIMSELF INTO TROUBLE.
   ISBN 978-1-4677-3272-7 (LIB. BDG. : ALK. PAPER)
   ISBN 978-1-4677-3274-1 (EBOOK)
   1. GRAPHIC NOVELS. [1. GRAPHIC NOVELS. 2. MARTIAL ARTS–FICTION. 3. SAMURAI–FICTION. 4. SCHOOLS–FICTION. 5. BEHAVIOR–FICTION.] I. RYSER, NICOLAS, ILLUSTRATOR. II. GAUVIN, EDWARD, TRANSLATOR. III. TITLE.
PZ7.7.R5NIN 2014
741.5'944–DC23   2013029022

MANUFACTURED IN THE UNITED STATES OF AMERICA
1 - VI - 12/31/13

The Search for Wisdom Crushes the Disciple Underfoot

YAAAAAA

GN NNG GNN

GN GNGNN

NGNN

GNN GN

TAO, DROP MY BARRETTES RIGHT NOW!

CLIK

A Samurai Is Sensitive to Color Combinations

OH, NO!

NO-NO-NO-NO-NO!

EEEEW! THAT'S SO HORRIBLE!

LATER...

HERE'S YOUR DVD BACK, TAO.

THERE'S SOME NASTY STUFF IN THERE.

LIKE AT THE BEGINNING, RIGHT?

NO, NO--

WHEN THE BIG GUY GETS BEHEADED? OR THE OLD GUY GETS CRUSHED UNDER THE TEMPLE?

NO, NOT THAT.

OR WHEN THE THREE SUPERLIZARDS GET GUTTED...OR THE THREE NINJAS GET AMBUSHED IN THEIR SLEEP--

NO!

JUST LOOK AT THE HERO'S KIMONO! THERE ARE THREE SCENES WHERE HE WEARS THIS GREEN THING WITH THOSE REVOLTING BROWN PANTS! BLECH!

?

The Samurai Who Seeks His Model Finds His Mirror

HERE'S TODAY'S LITTLE EXERCISE: IMAGINE YOURSELF AS AN ANIMAL AS YOU WORK ON YOUR KUNG FU POSES.

CRANE FIST

HERE HE GOES WITH THOSE ANIMALS AGAIN!

HEY, BRUCE LEE!

MEOM MEOM

NUM NUM

NUM NUM

OOOOAAA

MAN, I'M TIRED!

OOOOAA

ZZZ

Z Z Z

MMMMM

MMEOW

MIAM

SLURP

MIAM

CE LEE

Z Z Z Z

Z Z Z Z

TAO, NO OFFENSE TO OLD BRUCE LEE, BUT I DON'T THINK HE'S THE BEST MODEL TO FOLLOW!

HUH?

MEOW?

Missing the Mark

WHAT? LEE HAS TO DROP OUT?

WE'LL HAVE TO GET A SUBSTITUTE.

MASTER, I'LL GO FIND TAO!

SNOW DOJO 123

CHAN DOJO 121

TCHAK

HE'LL BE SO HAPPY!

AT LEAST *HE* WILL.

AN HOUR LATER...

LADIES AND GENTLEMEN, WE HAVE A WINNER! SNOW DOJO BY A HAIR...

CLAP CLAP CLAP CLAP CLAP CLAP CLAP CLAP CLAP

AH, MASTER IRONS! CONGRATULATIONS ON YOUR WIN. ALL WENT WELL?

UH...SORT OF A FEW OF TAO'S SHOTS WENT...

...A BIT WIDE!

A True Spy Is Not Afraid to Get His Feet Wet

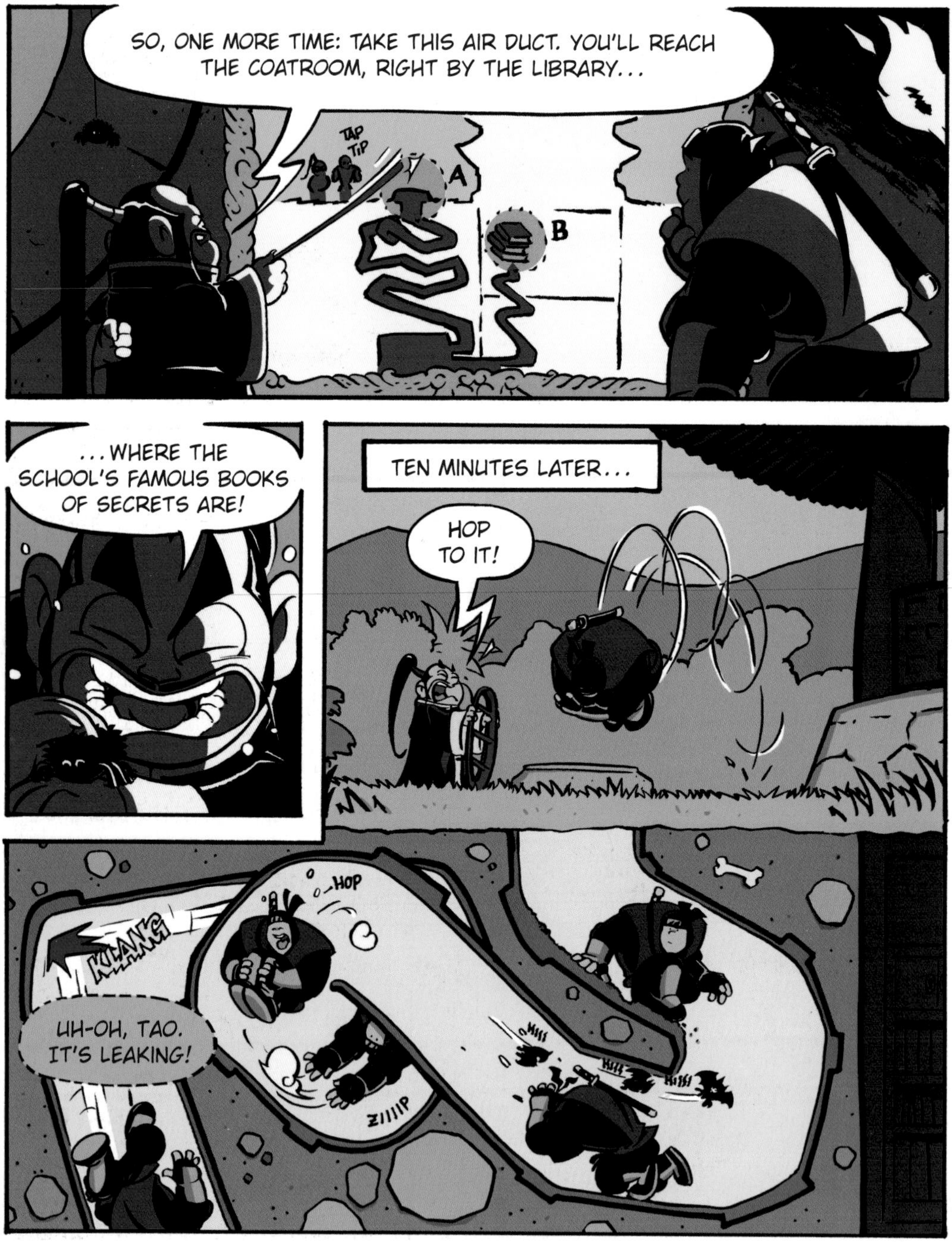
SO, ONE MORE TIME: TAKE THIS AIR DUCT. YOU'LL REACH THE COATROOM, RIGHT BY THE LIBRARY...
TAP TIP
A
B
...WHERE THE SCHOOL'S FAMOUS BOOKS OF SECRETS ARE!
TEN MINUTES LATER...
HOP TO IT!
HOP
KLANG
UH-OH, TAO. IT'S LEAKING!
HISS
ZIIIP

HURRY, SHUT THE TAP! UH-OH. IT'S NOT WORKING!

LET'S PRY THIS THING OFF. WE HAVE TO DRAIN THE WATER.

NGN... GNN GN!... GNA!

TAKING OUR PLUMBING TO MAKE BLOWPIPES? ARE YOU CRAZY?

A Samurai's Instincts Cannot Always Be Trusted

The Wise Man Reflects, the Madman Climbs

Silent Night, Quiet Reading

The True Samurai Knows No Fear (Mostly)

EVERYTHING'S GOING WELL!

INDEED!

DON'T GET UPSET, MASTER!

SNOW DOJO — VISITORS
028 000

THAT OLD MUTT SNOW HAS MADE FOOLS OF US AGAIN!

GRR! BLOOPER, GO ROUGH UP OUR NEXT OPPONENT A LITTLE...

A CERTAIN... TAO!

RIGHT AWAY, MASTER!

HEH HEH. A LITTLE ACCIDENT IS ON ITS WAY!

WHAT FRUIT DID YOU GET?

LATER...

AH! AT LAST!

DRAGON'S BREATH! THAT KID DID THIS TO YOU?

NOT EXACTLY...

I SLIPPED AND FELL...

TAO! RAY! YOUR TURN!

AND PICK UP YOUR TRASH! IT'S ALL OVER THE STAIRS!

 # Missing the Mark...Again

WITH MY BOKEN* IN HAND, THESE BAMBOO STALKS DON'T STAND A CHANCE!

YAHA

VLANK

NOT A SCRATCH!

I KNOW...

NEED A RUNNING START.

GO!

YAA

PAF

NOT BAD, TAO! NICE AIM!

*BOKEN: A WOODEN PRACTICE SWORD

Can't Beat Sense into a Dummy

A Grasshopper Who Learns Beats a Grasshopper Who Copies

TAO! LET GO! THERE'S TOO MUCH WIND!

DON'T WORRY! IT'S ALL UNDER CONTROL!

RIIIIGHT! AS USUAL!

SEE?

BAF

SHOULDA LET GO!

NO WORRIES, I ANCHORED IT WELL.

REALLY?

AAA AAAAAAAAA

EEEEEE

Love's Light Shines at Night

OH, NO! OH, NO!

RAY! RAY!

WAKE UP, RAY! RIGHT NOW, HURRY!

VLAM

I...I THINK THERE'S A HUGE PROBLEM--

WITH KAT!

HUH? IS SHE OK? WHAT'S WRONG? C'MON, SPILL!

...

I THINK I'M IN LOVE WITH HER!

Nothing Surprises a Know-It-All

Shared Happiness May Not Be Double Happiness

The Wise Man Chooses His Path Wisely

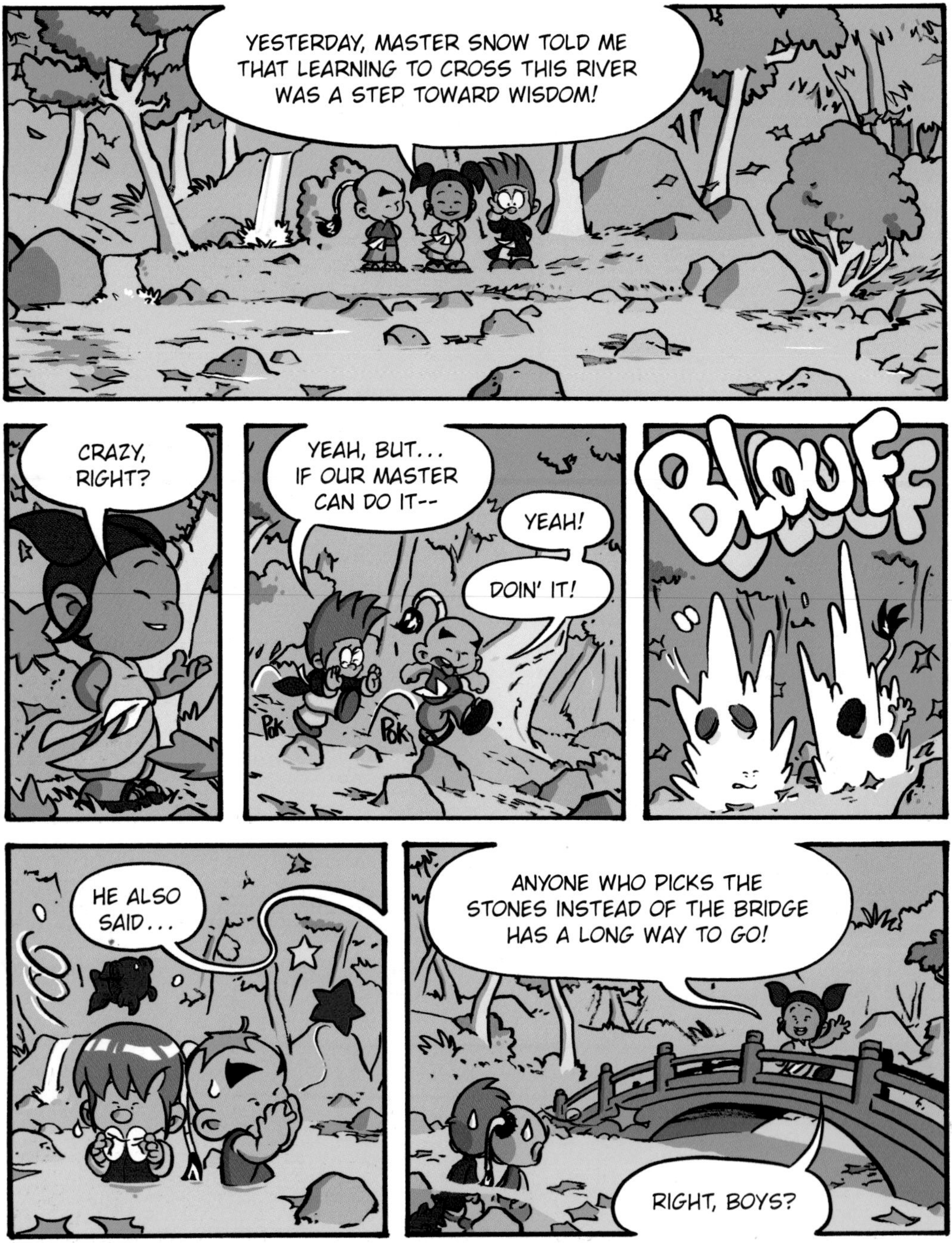

YESTERDAY, MASTER SNOW TOLD ME THAT LEARNING TO CROSS THIS RIVER WAS A STEP TOWARD WISDOM!
CRAZY, RIGHT?
YEAH, BUT... IF OUR MASTER CAN DO IT--
YEAH!
DOIN' IT!
POK
POK
BLOUFF
HE ALSO SAID...
ANYONE WHO PICKS THE STONES INSTEAD OF THE BRIDGE HAS A LONG WAY TO GO!
RIGHT, BOYS?

Everyone's a Critic

TAO! **VLAM**

DID YOU PUT WHITE-OUT ON ALL MY SAMURAI KIVAO MANGAS?

WELL? EVERY TIME KIVAO SHOWS UP, HE'S ALL WHITED-OUT!

UH...

CALM DOWN, KAT! I'M NOT DONE YET!

LOOK! I DREW MYSELF IN ALL OF KIVAO'S POSES! I WAS GONNA CUT 'EM OUT AND PASTE 'EM IN THE MANGAS!

AH...I GUESSH ISH NOT A GOOD IDEA...

Pranks and Planks

WHY HAVE YOU BEEN GIGGLING TO YOURSELF FOR THE LAST 10 MINUTES?

HEE HEE!

I PUT STICKY GREASE ON LEE AND KAT'S BOARDS! THEY'LL MESS UP THEIR KIMONOS!

GO AHEAD.

YOU'LL SEE! WE'LL HAVE A GOOD LAUGH!

YA!

KRAK

SBLURP

KROK

AYA!

YEP! LAUGHING MY HEAD OFF...

?

An Old Master's Cutting Remarks

STUDENTS, MAY I INTRODUCE MASTER STEELY BLADE. HE'S HERE TO GIVE A DEMONSTRATION.

EXCUSE ME, BUT UH...WHAT CAN THIS OLD GUY TEACH US?

KNITTING? CROCHET? WATERCOLORS?

SIGH...

YAAOOU

KWAK

OOOOUUU

YA YA YA YA

OH, RIGHT... SWORDSMANSHIP. OK!

Like Son, Like Father

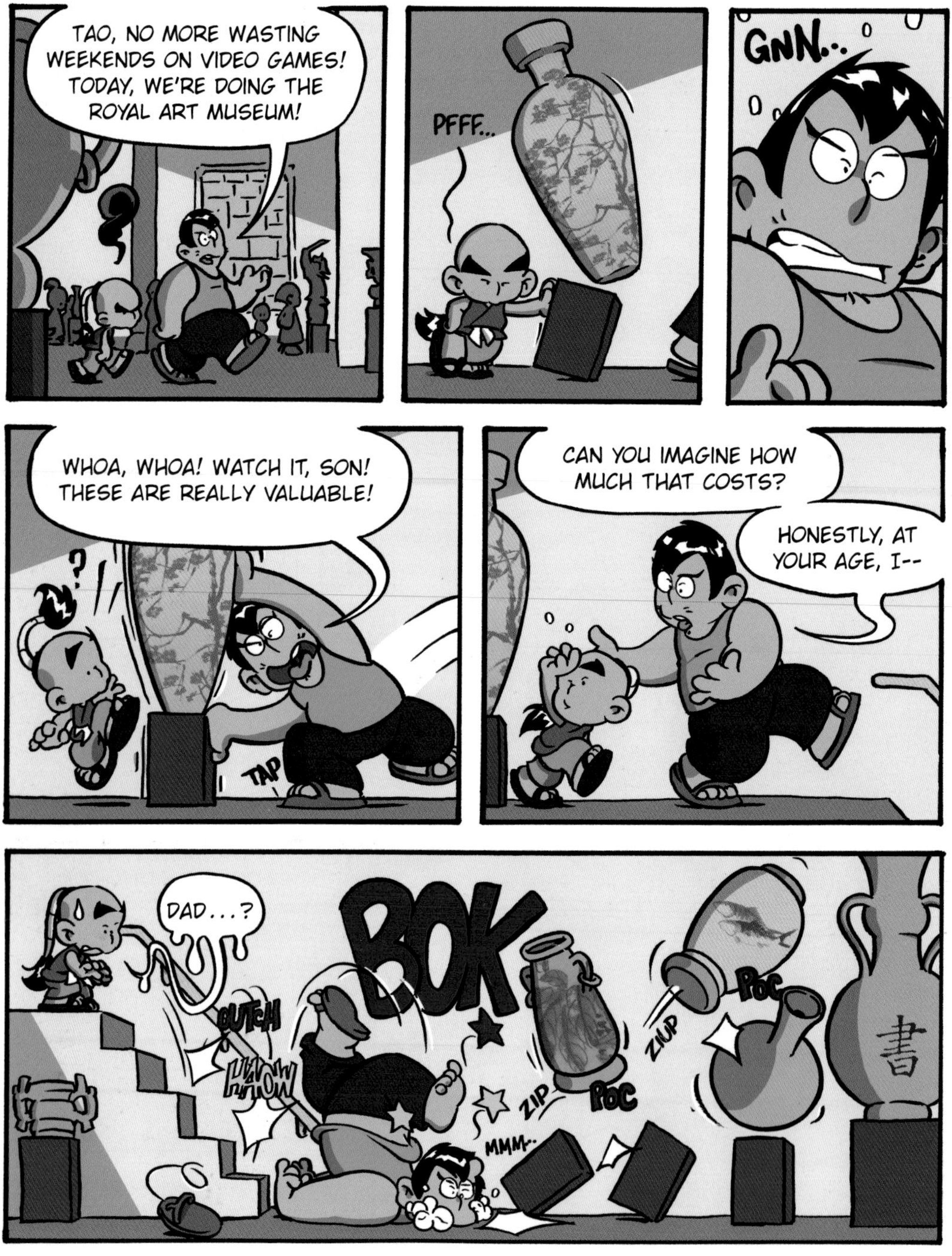

TAO, NO MORE WASTING WEEKENDS ON VIDEO GAMES! TODAY, WE'RE DOING THE ROYAL ART MUSEUM!
PFFF...
GNN...
WHOA, WHOA! WATCH IT, SON! THESE ARE REALLY VALUABLE!
TAP
CAN YOU IMAGINE HOW MUCH THAT COSTS?
HONESTLY, AT YOUR AGE, I--
DAD...?
BOK
OUTCH
HAOW
ZIP
POC
ZIUP
POC
MMM..

The Way of Water

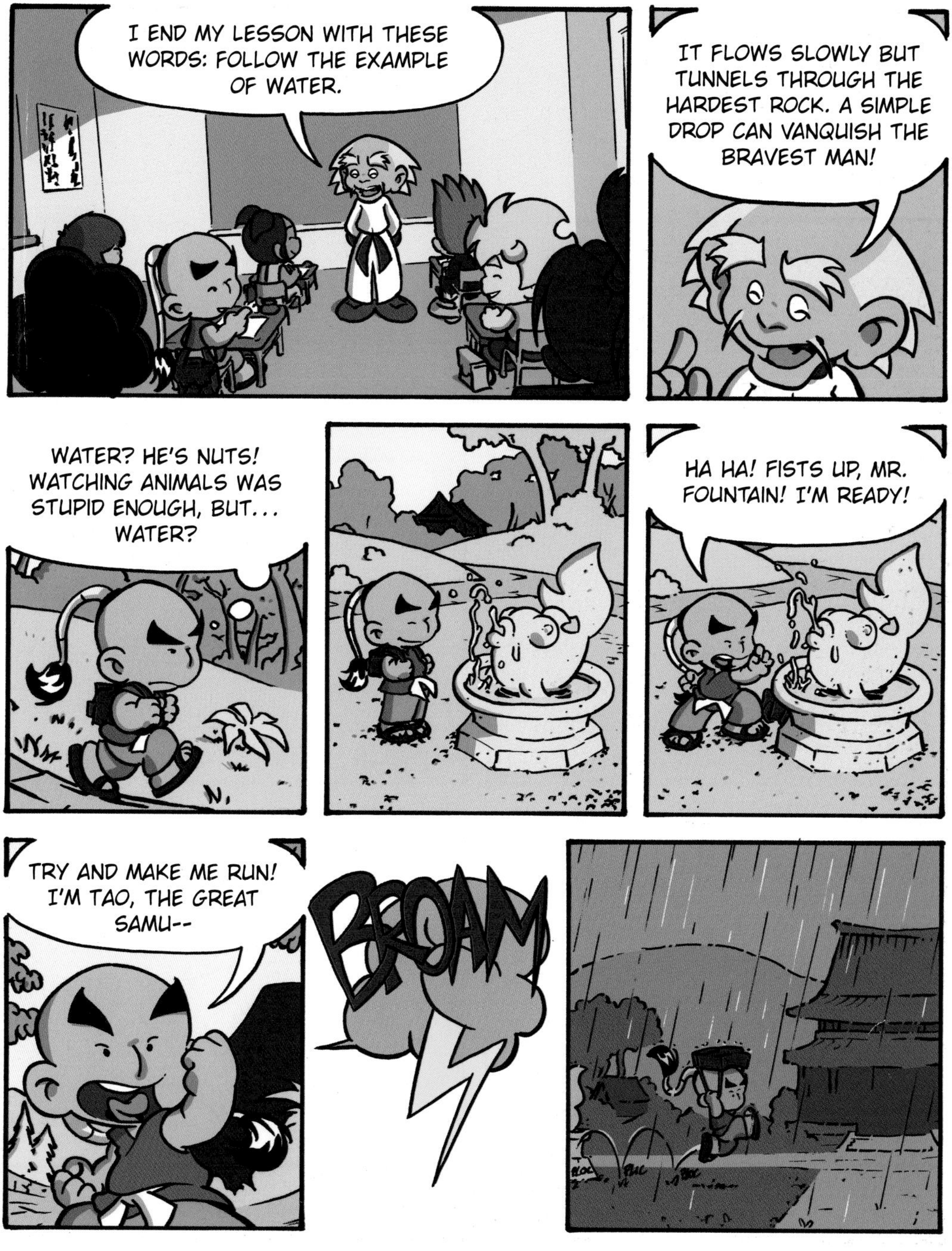
I END MY LESSON WITH THESE WORDS: FOLLOW THE EXAMPLE OF WATER.
IT FLOWS SLOWLY BUT TUNNELS THROUGH THE HARDEST ROCK. A SIMPLE DROP CAN VANQUISH THE BRAVEST MAN!
WATER? HE'S NUTS! WATCHING ANIMALS WAS STUPID ENOUGH, BUT... WATER?
HA HA! FISTS UP, MR. FOUNTAIN! I'M READY!
TRY AND MAKE ME RUN! I'M TAO, THE GREAT SAMU--
BROAM

The Road to Knowledge Is Long

I SIGNED YOU ALL UP FOR THREE-DAY COURSES WITH SPECIALISTS OVER VACATION.

YOU'LL BE LEARNING NEW SKILLS BEFORE BREAK!

COOL! I WONDER WHAT'S IN STORE. KATANA? BO STAFF?

THE NEXT DAY, FOR RAY

AWESOME! NUNCHAKU* TRAINING!

OOOUUH...

*TWO STICKS CONNECTED AT ONE END WITH A SHORT CHAIN OR ROPE

FOR KAT

EXCELLENT! A PENCAK SILAT* CLASS!

*AN INDONESIAN MARTIAL ART

FOR LEE

BO-JUTSU*! LOVE IT!

*THE ART OF THE BO STAFF

AND TAO

HEY, KID! HEARD YOU HAVE TROUBLE WITH YOUR BELT!

HUH? KNOT TYING?

A Rolling Grasshopper Gathers No Moss

GUYS! CLEAR THE ROAD!

TAO'S GONNA BE HERE ANY SECOND! SAVE YOURSELVES!

SO WHAT? WHY WOULD WE WANT TO DITCH TAO?

DON'T WORRY!

SURE, HE'S KIND OF A PAIN SOMETIMES, BUT--

NO, THAT'S-- I MEAN, I-- BUT--

HE'S--

OOUAA!

BABOOM

ON SKATES!

The Ultimate Challenge

HEY, MUNCHKINS. SHOULDN'T YOU BE REVIEWING YOUR BEGINNERS' KATAS?

NO, WE CAME TO CHALLENGE YOU!

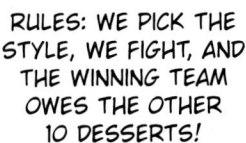

RULES: WE PICK THE STYLE, WE FIGHT, AND THE WINNING TEAM OWES THE OTHER 10 DESSERTS!

HA HA! FUNNY, SHRIMP! YOU'VE GOT NO CHANCE, BUT WHATEVS!

SO... DEAL?

DEAL!

SO WHAT WILL IT BE? KARATE? JUDO?

NO...

THE LATEST VERSION OF **SAMURAI ATTACK!**

UH...

WELL...

LOOK, MR. SUPERINTENDENT-- WINTER'S ENDING, AND OUR GARDEN IS COMING BACK TO LIFE.

I'M TREMBLING WITH EXCITEMENT!

THESE FAMOUS FLOWERS YOU LOVE SO MUCH JUST BLOSSOMED!

AH! WONDERFUL! NOTHING COULD PLEASE ME MORE!

THEY'RE OVER HERE, IN THESE BIG--

SWEET SKILLETS! THEY'RE ALL GONE!

WH-WHAT THE--?!

SHE LOVES ME NOT! I LOSE AGAIN!

I CAN'T BELIEVE THIS! ONE MORE TIME. KAT LOVES ME...

A Samurai Must Suffer for His Looks

NICE TRAINING SESSION! I'M BEAT!

YEAH, I'M ALL SWEATY!

SURE ARE! YOU STINK!

PEE-YEW!

HEY LOOK! IT'S KAT AND MIMI.

HUH? WHAT? WHO'S GOT DEODORANT? HURRY, GUYS!

QUICK, THEY'RE COMING! HURRY!

PLOUTCH

TAO, NO--

WHAT?

HEY, BOYS!

WHAT TH--

MY VOLUMIZING SHAMPOO!

WHAT?

HA HA HA HA HA HA HA HA HA

Artistry vs. Allergies

GAZE UPON THESE SPLENDID BONSAIS, SON--BUT DON'T TOUCH A THING!

YES, DAD.

EVER SINCE IT FLOWERED, THIS ONE'S BEEN THE PRIDE OF THE MUSEUM!

GREAT...

OOH! WHAT A STRONG SMELL!

GNNN...

AHHH...

ATCHOO

I DIDN'T TOUCH IT, I SWEAR!

# Moving Mountains with Your Mind

GOTTA HAND IT TO MASTER SNOW--HE'S A CHAMPION AT LEVITATION!

BUT IT'S JUST A MATTER OF CONCENTRATING!

CLEARING YOUR MIND AND FOCUSING!

OK, LET'S TRY AGAIN. CONCENTRATE!

MMGNN...

IT WORKED THIS TIME!

WHAT--

LOOK, IF YOU'RE GONNA KEEP DISTRACTING ME--

?

# The Fisherman Must Not Fear Getting Wet

35

Nitpickers Can Be Such a Nuisance

THESE ARE THE BASIC TAI-CHI STANCES.

REMEMBER, THESE MOVEMENTS SHOULD BE MADE SLOWLY AND GENTLY!

YAA

NGN NG 'N GN

YA YA YA YA YA

TAO, WHAT IN THE WORLD IS THAT? IT'S WAY TOO FAST!

YAY NGN Y

SORRY, MISTRESS LAKE, BUT I HAD A SLUG IN MY KIMONO!

# The Adventurous Dragon Is Ever Watchful

LISTEN UP, KIDS! THIS JUNGLE CAN BE DANGEROUS.

STAY CLOSE AND DON'T LEAVE THE TRAIL!

YA! YÉ!

GOT IT? LET'S GO!

HALF AN HOUR LATER...

MAN, WHAT A LONG WALK!

MMMR...

STRANGE...WHERE'D KAT GO?

RAY, CAN YOU HEAR ME?

MMMRR...

I THINK WE'RE LOST!

SIGH...THESE HIKES ARE SO BORING! YOU NEVER SEE A THING!

MMMR...

Tao, the Little Samurai

The Dragon's Belly Laugh

 # A Student's Face Is an Open Book

HEY, TUCK!

EVENING, TAO.

DONE WITH CLASS FOR TODAY?

YEAH--IT WAS GREAT! YOU'LL NEVER GUESS WHAT MISTRESS LAKE TAUGHT US!

A CALLIGRAPHY CLASS?

NO WAY! HOW'D YOU GUESS?

HEH HEH...

# The Way of Lee

TAO, YOU SHOULD REALLY READ MORE!

YEAH...

GRAND GARDENS

BOOKS ARE IMPORTANT! YOU CAN FIND EVERYTHING IN THEM! EVEN A PURPOSE IN LIFE!

THE GREAT THINKERS OF THE PAST HELP US WITH THEIR VALUABLE ADVICE!

BOOKS WILL HELP YOU FIND YOUR PATH!

THE WAY FORWARD...

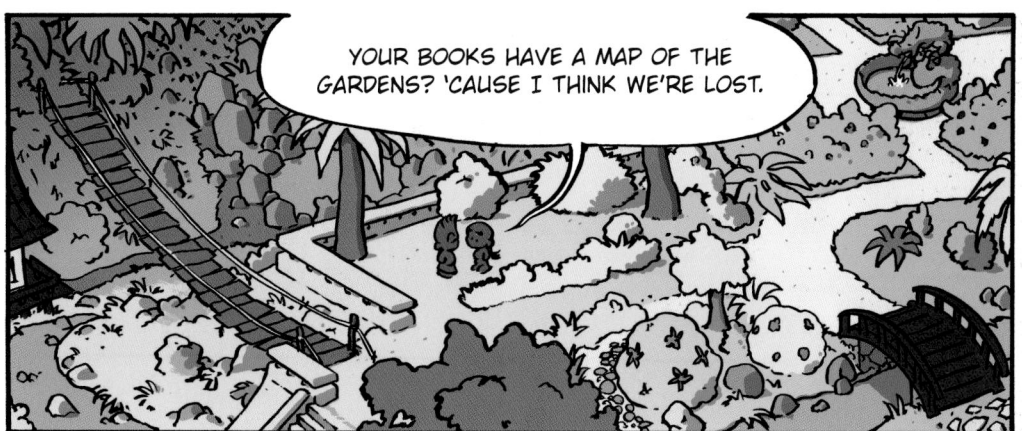

YOUR BOOKS HAVE A MAP OF THE GARDENS? 'CAUSE I THINK WE'RE LOST.

He Who Steals a Candle Ends Up Burned

MAN, THIS IS GONNA BE A GREAT PARTY!

YEAH!

SURE WILL! THE GREAT CANDLE FESTIVAL IS A SCHOOL TRADITION!

GRR...

THAT STUPID FESTIVAL ALWAYS DRAWS CROWDS TO THAT FOSSIL SNOW!

BLOOPER, TIME TO PROCEED WITH OUR PLAN. BRING ME AS MANY CANDLES AS YOU CAN!

THE MASTER'S PLAN IS FOOLPROOF! WITHOUT CANDLES, THE PARTY'S A BUST!

WOOSH

MASTER SNOW! SOMEONE STOLE ALL THE CANDLES FROM THE GARDEN!

STRANGE, KAT...WE HAVEN'T LAID OUT CANDLES YET. TUCK WILL START SOON.

OH. BUT STILL--

DON'T WORRY. FOR NOW, JUST LEND ME A HAND.

OK.

SIGH...

YOU THINK THEY KNEW ABOUT THE SURPRISE FIREWORKS IN THE GARDEN?

DRAGON'S BREATH! I'LL GET YOU SOMEDAY!

Grasshopper First Responder

OH, NO! I'M GONNA BE LATE TO THE LESSON AGAIN!

AAAH! WHAT DO I DO? WHAT DO I DO? HELP HELP... HELP

WHO DO I CALL? GOTTA STAY COOL. GOTTA BE BRAVE. THINK, TAO...

HURRY UP! DO SOMETHING...

YOU WERE RIGHT: I THINK TAO'S NOT READY FOR OUR FIRST AID LESSON YET!

Speediness Is Next to Carelessness

A Warrior's Vacation Is Never Restful

AH, SPEARFISHING! NOW THERE'S A SPORT! NOT LIKE FISHING WITH TUCK!

CAREFUL, NOW...

THERE!

TCHAK

AHHAAA

TAO! WHAT WERE YOU THINKING?

ULP! MASTER IRONS! WHAT ARE YOU DOING HERE?

FLAP! FLAP FLIP

A Samurai's Memory Is like an Elephant's

LEE GOT HIS FIRST BAD GRADE! AN F, I SWEAR!

IT'S SURE TO BRING HIS GRADE POINT DOWN!

HA!

AND DID YOU HEAR VUVU GOT THIS WEIRD RASH?

UH-HUH! HER WHOLE BELLY'S YELLOW!

NO...

REALLY?

SHE'S GOT BAD ALLERGIES!!

AND KEN'S GOING OUT WITH THIS TALL GIRL FROM SIXTH GRADE! DID YOU HEAR?

OOOOOH!

DID YOU NOTICE KAT'S NEW OUTFIT? KINDA WEIRD, RIGHT?

TOTALLY WEIRD!

HAH! EVEN WEIRDER: TUCK'S FLOWER-PRINT UNDERWEAR!

YEAH! TOTALLY!

HELLO, CHILDREN. HOW ARE YOUR CLASSES GOING?

WELL...IT'S NOT EASY! THERE'S SO MUCH TO MEMORIZE!

 # A Samurai Takes Advantage of His Opponent's State of Mind

 # A Wise Man Always Finds the Right Words

WELL...TIME TO DO MY GRADING!

TAO...HMM...HAVE TO TRY AND FIND SOMETHING POSITIVE TODAY.

UMM...

YIIIPPEEE!

THAT'S IT!

TAO IS ALWAYS ON TIME FOR LUNCH.

The Sweeter the Dream, the Harder the Fall

He Who Would See Far Must First Rise High

One Too Many Really Is Too Many

NO PRACTICE THIS AFTERNOON! WE CAN RELAX!

TAO'S NOT HERE! WE CAN WATCH THE LATEST KIVAO IF YOU WANT.

YEAH! GREAT IDEA!

AWESOME!

HURRY UP!

BEFORE HE COMES!

TEN MINUTES LATER...

YAHCLING HOO-Y

HEY, GUYS!

YOU GUYS WATCHING KIVAO? I'LL JOIN YOU!

UH--

WELL--

WE JUST--

YEAH! HIT 'IM!

AWESOME!

GO GET 'EM!

A Samurai Must Have a Sharp Eye

GUYS, GUYS! I MADE THE COVER OF MARTIAL ARTS MAGAZINE!

HUH? WHAT? THE COVER?

TOTALLY!

LEMME SEE...

?

NO WAY!

WHAT?! THAT'S NOT YOU ON THE COVER?

SURE IT IS! IN THE THIRD ROW!

MARTIAL ARTS MAG

MUSCLE JOE

TAP TAP

yeah!

AYAAA HIIII

LOOK OUT! THE EMPIRE'S NINJAS ARE BACK!

THE KINGS OF NUNCHAKU!

ONE BLOW FROM THIS WEAPON CAN KNOCK OUT A DRAGON!

WIIIIPP

WAAAP

WOOUP

??

RAY! TAO! COME BACK HERE AT ONCE!

GIVE BACK THOSE SAUSAGES YOU STOLE! RIGHT NOW!

STRATEGIC RETREAT, NINJA TAO!

NIKO & LOLO

The Creators of Tao Give Tips on Drawing Tao!

C'MON BACKSTAGE AND SEE THINGS FROM THE OTHER SIDE!

TODAY WE'VE DECIDED TO GIVE YOU A FEW TIPS ON DRAWING!

RIGHT, NIKO?

MMHMM...

RIGHT...OK, I'LL START!

SCRITCH

WHEN WE DESIGN A CHARACTER, WE HAVE TO PICK A SHAPE FIRST!

TAO, FOR EXAMPLE...

...IS LIKE AN APPLE.

COOL! I NEEDED A SNACK!

DON'T EAT THAT! I'M EXPLAINING HOW TO DRAW TAO!

CRUNCH!

GULP! TOO LATE!

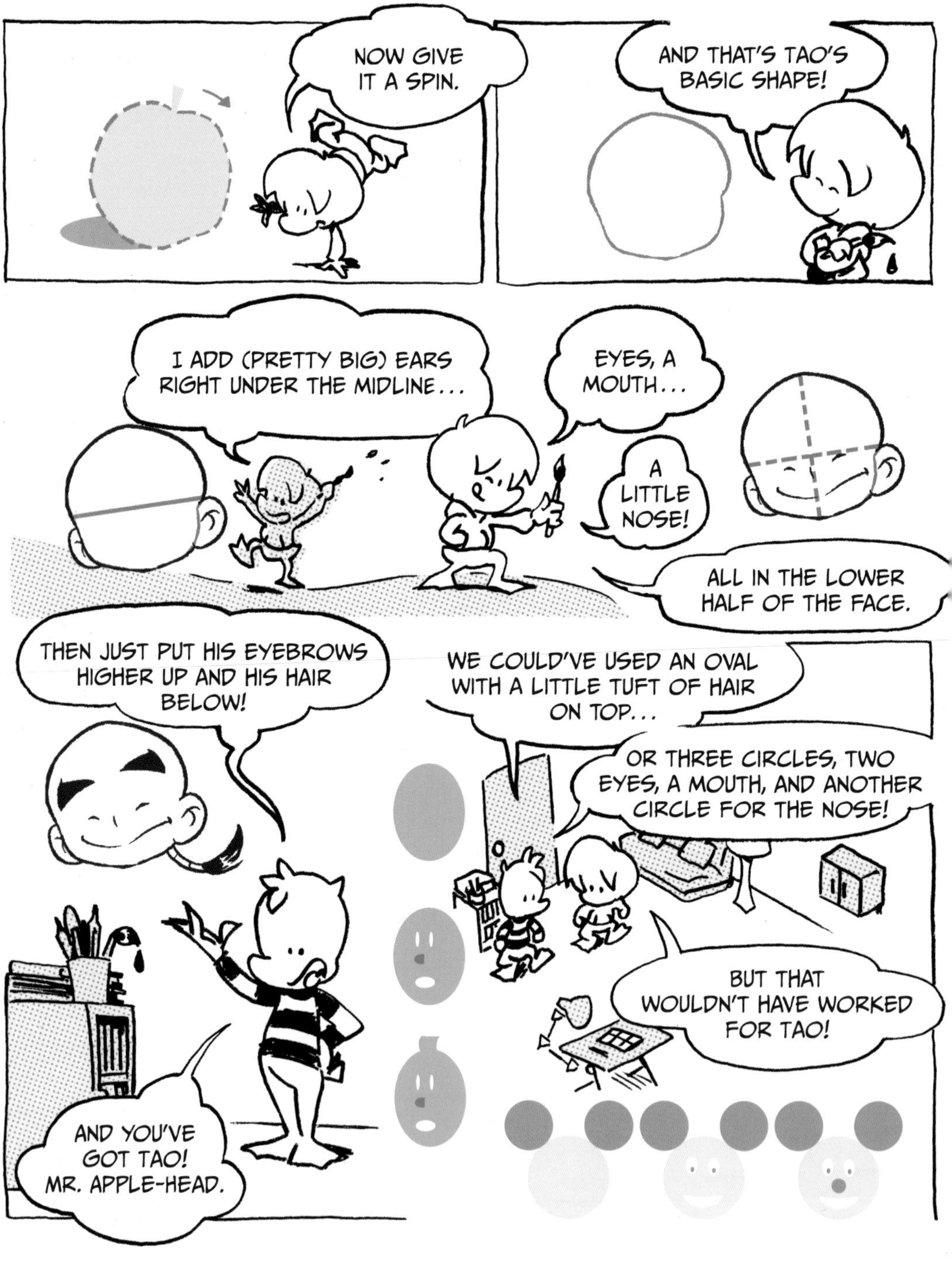
NOW GIVE IT A SPIN.
AND THAT'S TAO'S BASIC SHAPE!
I ADD (PRETTY BIG) EARS RIGHT UNDER THE MIDLINE...
EYES, A MOUTH...
A LITTLE NOSE!
ALL IN THE LOWER HALF OF THE FACE.
THEN JUST PUT HIS EYEBROWS HIGHER UP AND HIS HAIR BELOW!
AND YOU'VE GOT TAO! MR. APPLE-HEAD.
WE COULD'VE USED AN OVAL WITH A LITTLE TUFT OF HAIR ON TOP...
OR THREE CIRCLES, TWO EYES, A MOUTH, AND ANOTHER CIRCLE FOR THE NOSE!
BUT THAT WOULDN'T HAVE WORKED FOR TAO!

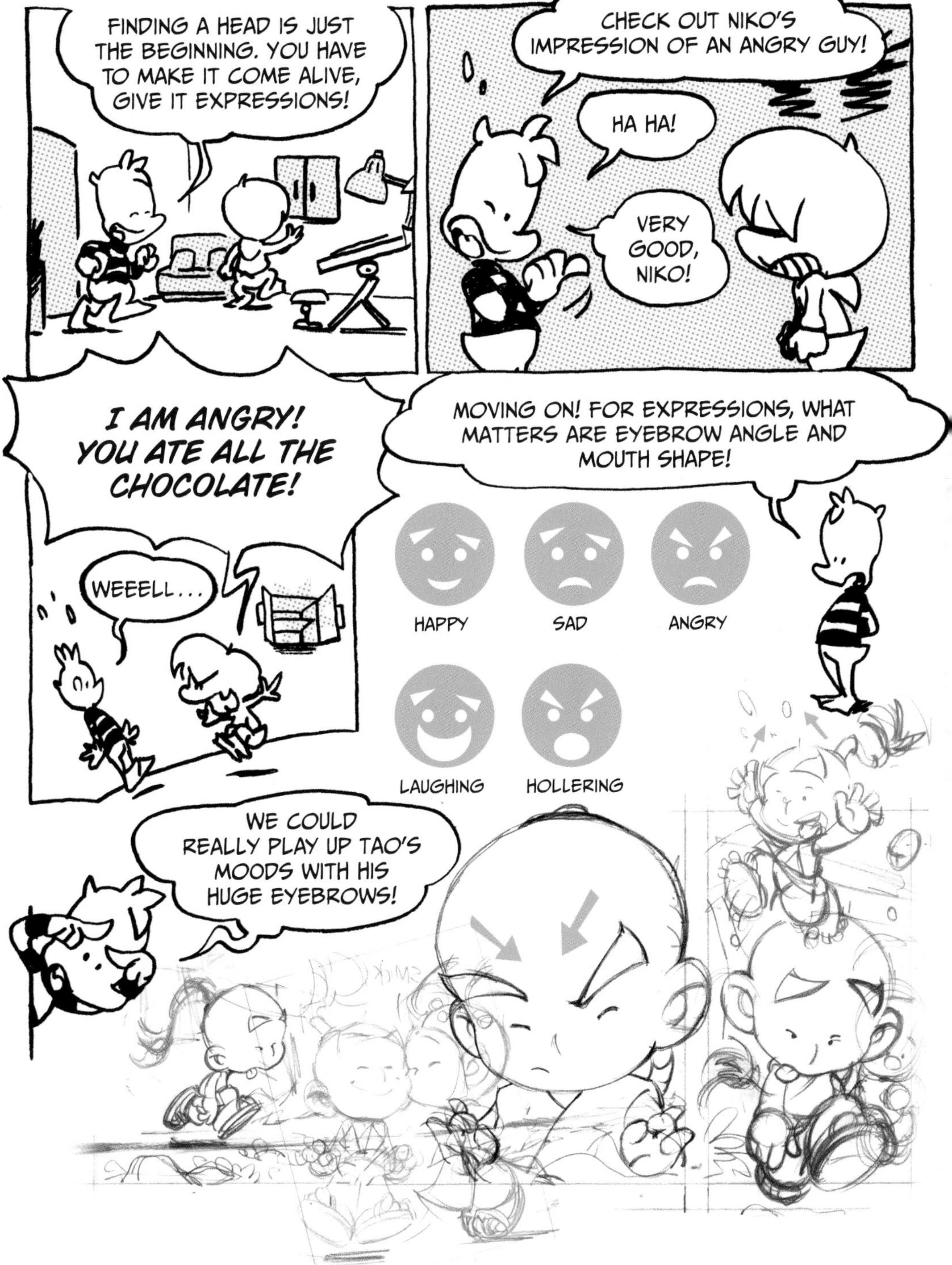

FINDING A HEAD IS JUST THE BEGINNING. YOU HAVE TO MAKE IT COME ALIVE, GIVE IT EXPRESSIONS!
CHECK OUT NIKO'S IMPRESSION OF AN ANGRY GUY!
HA HA!
VERY GOOD, NIKO!
I AM ANGRY! YOU ATE ALL THE CHOCOLATE!
WEEELL...
MOVING ON! FOR EXPRESSIONS, WHAT MATTERS ARE EYEBROW ANGLE AND MOUTH SHAPE!
HAPPY
SAD
ANGRY
LAUGHING
HOLLERING
WE COULD REALLY PLAY UP TAO'S MOODS WITH HIS HUGE EYEBROWS!

OF COURSE, A HEAD WITHOUT A BODY IS HARDLY ALIVE.

TO DRAW A BODY, YOU HAVE TO MEASURE OUT PROPORTIONS. THAT MEANS THE SIZE OF DIFFERENT PARTS COMPARED TO EACH OTHER.

WE USE THE HEAD AS A UNIT OF MEASURE.

IN TAO, OUR HERO IS ABOUT TWO HEADS TALL.

THE ADULTS ARE ABOUT 4½ HEADS.

SCRITCH SCRATCH

1
2
3
4
4,5

A MORE REALISTIC CHARACTER WOULD BE DIFFERENT: AROUND 7 OR 8 HEADS TALL.

WHO ARE THOSE TWO CLOWNS?

FINALLY, WE HAVE TO MAKE OUR CHARACTERS MOVE!

HOP HOP

THERE'S A LITTLE TRICK WE USE: PICTURE A WIRE PUPPET!

IT'S EASIER TO GET AN IDEA OF HOW HE MOVES.

HOP

BING

RUNNING, DIVING, KICKING...

THEN WE DRAW AROUND THESE POINTS!

SCRATCH

GUESS WHAT?
NOW IT'S YOUR TURN!

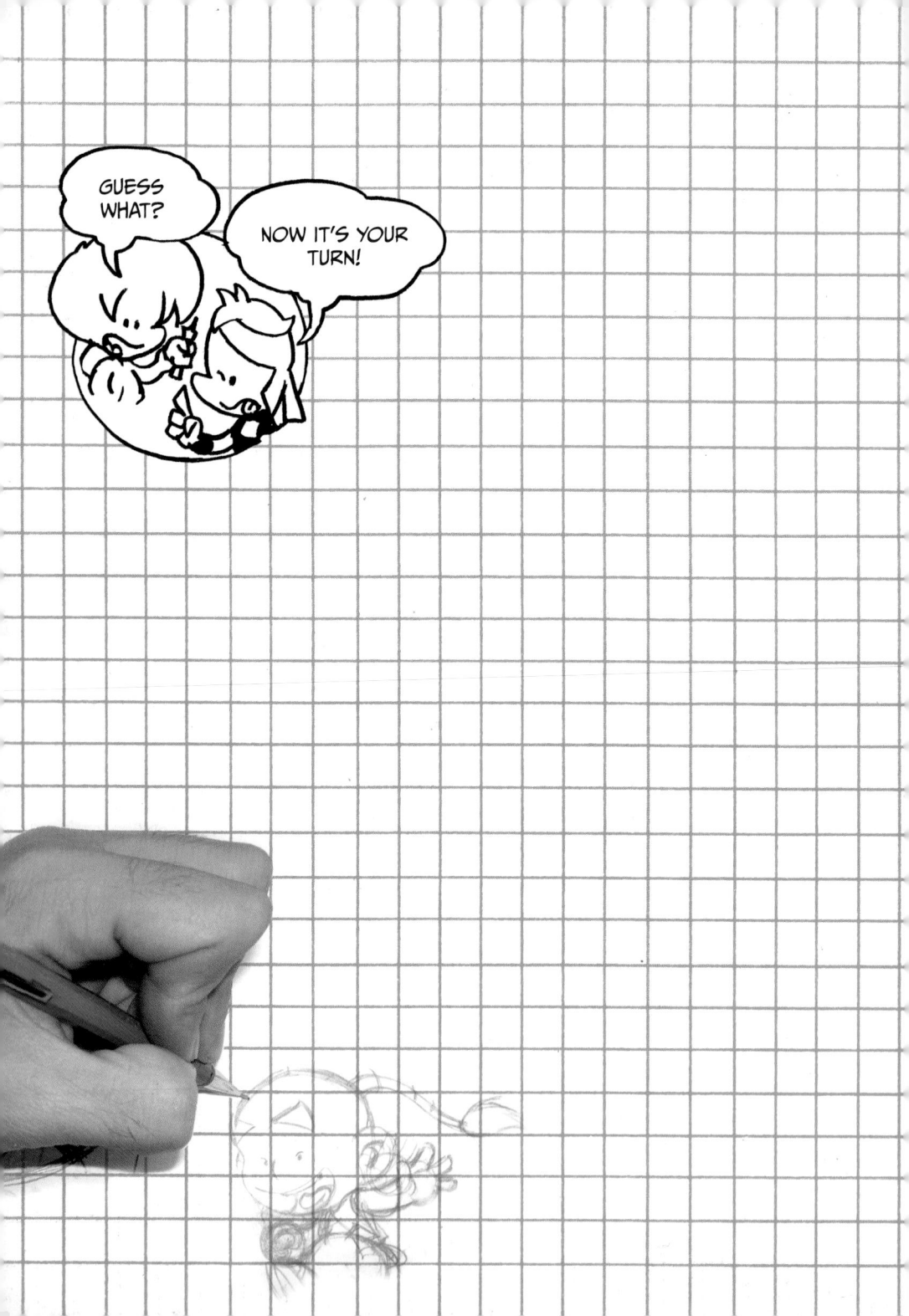

TAO
The Little Samurai

#1 Pranks and Attacks!
#2 Ninjas and Knock Outs!
#3 Clowns and Dragons!